I Love You Because You're You

This book belongs to:

_____

I Love You
Because
You're You

ISBN 978-0-439-20656-3

17 16 15 14 13 12 11 10 9 8   15 16 17 18 19 20/0

Printed in China   95

I Love You Because You're You

by Liza Baker

Illustrated by
David McPhail

SCHOLASTIC INC.

New York   Toronto   London   Auckland
Sydney   Mexico City   New Delhi   Hong Kong

I love you when you're happy
and grinning ear to ear.

I love you when you're sleepy
and want to snuggle near.

I love you when you're silly
and dancing 'round
and 'round.

I love you when you're frightened
and hear a scary sound.

I love you when you're bashful
and hide behind my knee.

I love you when you're brave,
and from my arms you flee.

I love you when you're curious
and searching here and there.

I love you when you're proud,
your head held in the air.

I love you when you're sick
and need to rest in bed.

I love you when you're frisky
and standing on your head.

I love you when you're sad
and need a kiss and hug.

I love you when you're playful
and rolling on the rug.

I love you when you're angry
and cross your arms and pout.

I love you when you're wild
and yell and scream and shout.

I love you
any way you feel,
no matter
what you do.

I love you
any way you are.

I love you
because
you're you!